A NOTE TO PARENTS

When your children are ready to "step into reading," giving them the right books is as crucial as giving them the right food to eat. **Step into Reading Books** present exciting stories and information reinforced with lively, colorful illustrations that make learning to read fun, satisfying, and worthwhile. They are priced so that acquiring an entire library of them is affordable. And they are beginning readers with a difference—they're written on five levels.

Early Step into Reading Books are designed for brand-new readers, with large type and only one or two lines of very simple text per page. **Step 1 Books** feature the same easy-to-read type as the Early Step into Reading Books, but with more words per page. **Step 2 Books** are both longer and slightly more difficult, while **Step 3 Books** introduce readers to paragraphs and fully developed plot lines. **Step 4 Books** offer exciting nonfiction for the increasingly independent reader.

The grade levels assigned to the five steps—preschool through kindergarten for the Early Books, preschool through grade 1 for Step 1, grades 1 through 3 for Step 2, grades 2 through 3 for Step 3, and grades 2 through 4 for Step 4—are intended only as guides. Some children move through all five steps very rapidly; others climb the steps over a period of several years. Either way, these books will help your child "step into reading" in style!

Published in the United States by Random House, Inc., New York, and simultaneously in Canada by Random House of Canada Limited, Toronto.

http://www.randomhouse.com/

Library of Congress Cataloging-in-Publication Data
Farber, Erica.
Ooey gooey / written by Erica Farber and J. R. Sansevere.
p. cm. — (Mercer Mayer's critters of the night) (Step into reading. A step 1 book)
SUMMARY: When Captain Short Bob, the pirate king, cooks up a dish of bubble gum and tuna fish, he loses his gold tooth to a sea beast.
ISBN 0-679-88991-4 (trade) — ISBN 0-679-98991-9 (lib. bdg.)
[1. Pirates—Fiction. 2. Teeth—Fiction. 3. Stories in rhyme.]
I. Sansevere, John R. II. Title III. Series: Step into reading. Step 1 book.
IV. Series: Critters of the night.
PZ7.F222750o 1998
[E]—dc21 97-40962

Printed in the United States of America 10 9 8 7 6 5 4 3 2 1

 A BIG TUNA TRADING COMPANY, LLC/J. R. SANSEVERE BOOK

Step into Reading®

MERCER MAYER'S

CRITTERS OF THE NIGHT®

OOEY GOOEY

Written by
Erica Farber and J. R. Sansevere

A Step 1 Book

Random House New York

Bones
See
Snake
Wanda
Jack
Thistle
Axel

Capt. Short Bob
Dracul Duck
Wolf Mouse

Groad Frankengator Moose Mummy

Uncle Mole Zombie Mombie Auntie Bell

Captain Short Bob,
the pirate king,
is not afraid
of anything.
He laughs at sharks
and big blue whales
and great sea beasts
with long, sharp tails.

He has a sword
he likes to hold
and a tooth
that's made of gold.

He has a boat.

It is his house.

He lives there with

his friend Wolf Mouse.

Wolf Mouse works hard.

He steers

and sails.

He scrubs the deck.

He looks
for whales.

Short Bob loves food.
Sometimes he cooks.
And while he cooks,
he reads cook books.

They searched the sand,
north, south, and east.
Searched everywhere.
Where was that beast?

They talked to crabs,
to shrimp and eels,
to starfish and
some baby seals.

They asked a shark.
They asked a whale.
But still no beast
with long, sharp tail.

That beast, that beast
just was not there.
He'd swum away.
He'd gone somewhere.

Now Short Bob eats
soup, mush, and stew.
For that is all
that he can chew.

He sails the seas
from west to east.
He looks and looks
for that sea beast.
Guess what Bob hates
with all his might?

Ooey gooey

pirate delight!